£4·95

NEW **Spirals**

FICTION

Sweet Dreams

John Townsend

Published in 2003 by:
Nelson Thornes Ltd
Delta Place
27 Bath Road
CHELTENHAM
GL53 7TH
United Kingdom

03   04   05   06   07   /   10   9   8   7   6   5   4   3   2   1

A catalogue record for this book is available from the British Library

ISBN 0 7487 7248 0

Cover illustration by Paul McCaffrey
Page make-up by Tech-Set, Gateshead

Printed in Croatia by Zrinski

1

Grey rain blew in off a grey sea. Grey spray swept over the grey pier. Lyn wiped the misty glass and peered out of the bus. A dull seaside town miles from home. This place had seen better days. All grey. Her heart sank.

The bus pulled up by the pier. 'That's it! The last stop. All get off here. Soggy-on-Sea!' The driver chuckled.

Lyn looked around the bus. She was the only one left on it. She took her bags down from the rack and made her way along the bus.

'Nice day for the beach, love!' the driver winked. 'Rather you than me.'

Lyn felt the cold wind bite at her arms. Gusts of rain stung her face. As soon as she got down on to the path, the doors closed with a hiss and the bus moved off. She stood alone in the fumes. Gloomy. Grim. Grey.

A tatty poster by the pier gates told her why she was there. It was already peeling off in the wet.

'SEASIDE SPECIAL. The best show in town!'

The show began in a few days. Rehearsals began tomorrow.

Lyn had got the job weeks ago at dance school. It all seemed great then. But now, as she looked down at the empty windswept beach, she wasn't so sure. As she looked at the grey hotels along the bleak sea front, she had second thoughts.

The smell of frying fish hung in the air. Lyn wanted to get in the dry and warm. She saw a café next to a slot-machine arcade. That would do.

She would buy a local paper to look at over a cup of coffee. She would find a guest house. Somewhere near the theatre.

She took her mobile phone from her handbag and swore. There wasn't a signal. Now she felt worse. She couldn't face being without her mobile. It hadn't let her down before.

At least there was a phone box by the pier. Perhaps there would be a *Yellow Pages* inside. There must be lots of guest houses nearby, she thought. She made her way to the phone box, but when she got there she swore again. The phone box was smashed. It was full of broken glass and the phone was missing. Her spirits sank even further. What a dump this place was.

A newspaper stand caught her eye. Large black letters said:

'ANOTHER TEENAGER MISSING.
POLICE SEARCH THE BEACH.'

This place is enough to make you go missing, thought Lyn. She'd been there two minutes and already she wanted to get away.

Lyn opened the café door. A few heads turned. 'Shut the door, love,' an old man shouted. 'There's a gale out there. We don't want it in here too!' Lyn did as she was told. She felt like shouting back but she bit her lip. What a grotty hole this is, she thought.

Lyn looked back at the rain. She had never felt so alone.

It was then that she felt a hand on her arm.

2

Lyn turned and looked up. The hand belonged to a young man. He was about 18. 'Hi!' he said. 'You look lost. I saw you get off the bus. You don't look very happy.'

'It's the rain,' she said. 'It's all a bit grim.'

'Yeah,' he said, 'it's not the best of places in the rain.'

'You can say that again. My mobile won't work and that phone out there is useless. It's not much of a welcome!'

The stranger smiled. 'Then I'd better see what I can do. Let me cheer you up. My name's Jed. Jed Hare. Come and have a coffee. It looks like you need one. There's a table in the corner.'

'Thanks. Er . . . I'm Lyn. Yeah, thanks.' Lyn went to the table and put her bags in the corner. Jed came with a tray, carrying two steaming mugs and a plate of buns. 'One thing they do well here,' he said, 'is these buns. Magic.'

He sat down and she smiled. 'Thanks.'

'So,' he said with a grin, 'what's a nice girl like you doing in a dump like this?'

'Showbiz. I sing and dance. I'm in the show here next week.'

'Wow. That's magic!'

'Not really. But it's my first proper job. I only left dance school last week.'

Jed took a huge bite of a bun. Lyn smiled. She felt better already. It was warm in here. All the windows were steamed up. It felt cosy. Chips sizzled and spat in the fryer.

Lyn blew on her coffee. 'So, what about you? What brings a good-looking lad like you to the seaside? Not fish and chips!'

Jed gulped his bun. He tapped his nose.

'Secret,' he whispered. 'I'm on the look-out.'

Lyn waited for him to say more. 'This . . .' he said. He took a rolled newspaper from his back pocket and threw it on the table. 'I'm looking for him.' Lyn saw the headline. ANOTHER TEENAGER MISSING. Jed took a gulp of coffee.

'My mate. It's Barry. He came here two weeks ago. He got a job at the holiday camp – in the bar. He'd only been there a day when . . . gone. Into thin air. That's not like Barry.'

'Maybe he met someone,' Lyn said and gave a smile.

'Oh yeah – he met someone all right. Like all the others round here who've gone missing. Someone up to no good. Someone downright evil if you ask me.'

3

The rain ran down the window in torrents. A string of plastic flags across the street flapped in the wind. A seagull dived at chip papers on the beach.

'I'm going to get soaked,' Lyn said. 'I've got to find somewhere to stay.'

'No problem,' Jed said. 'There are lots of places along the front. In fact, I'm staying at a B and B just up the road. It's not bad. It's got lots of empty rooms. Mrs Burke is OK. She's a bit weird but she's nice enough. You could come and see.'

Lyn thought. 'Yeah, maybe. I'll take a look.'

'Safety in numbers,' Jed whispered.

Lyn looked puzzled. 'What do you mean?'

'Well,' he began, tapping his nose again, 'I told the police but they don't agree. I've been looking into things. Did you know that hundreds of people disappear in this country every day? No one knows where they go. A lot are like you and me. They just go. Here one minute and gone the next. And this place . . .' He looked over his shoulder as if a net was about to whip him away. 'This place is the worst. More people have gone missing from this town in the last year than anywhere else. Not one of them has been found. Ever.'

'So where do you think they go? Little green aliens eat them?' Lyn drained her coffee mug.

'It's no joking matter. Listen. That's a clue.' They could hear a siren in the distance.

'Do you mean the police?' Lyn said. 'What have they got to do with it?'

Jed looked really serious now. He leaned forward. 'Not the police. Hospital. Have you ever heard of the famous hospital two miles away? And what's it famous for?'

'Er . . . I'm not sure . . .' Lyn said.

'Transplants,' Jed paused. 'Hundreds of them. Liver, heart, lungs . . . Any bits you need, they get them for you. But have you ever thought about where they get them from?'

Lyn laughed. 'Now you're winding me up!'

'No, I'm not. Listen. Hundreds of young people come to this town to work every summer. A lot of them are never seen again. I've been looking for Barry all week. Nothing. Dead ends all the time. I think there's a black market going on. In body parts. And if I were you, Lyn, I'd let me keep a close eye on you. A young healthy girl like you is just what they want. Trust me. I know what I'm saying.'

Lyn felt a shiver run down her spine.

4

Lyn liked Jed's smile. He cheered her up. Even though what he said scared her, his eyes had a real sparkle. She looked at the newspaper on the table.

'It says here that Barry James may have been washed out to sea after a late night swim.'

'Rubbish!' Jed spat a shower of crumbs on to his plate. 'Barry never swam. He'd never go near the water. I tell you, there's a body snatcher on the loose. Some rich people with worn out insides will pay the earth for new body parts.'

Lyn looked scared. Had she done the right thing coming here and taking this job? She'd been so pleased when she passed all the stage tests. She'd been so looking forward to being in her first big show. Now she wasn't so sure.

'Don't look so worried, Lyn,' he said. 'I'll look after you. If you stay at Mrs Burke's I'll be your personal bodyguard. Or should I say, body-parts guard!'

'How can I refuse?' she laughed.

The door opened with a cold blast of wet wind. 'Shut the door!' someone called. A policewoman shook rain from

her jacket and spoke to the man at the till. She showed
him a photo and wrote in a notebook. Then she came to
Lyn and Jed's table.

'I wonder if you can help?' she asked.

Jed spoke. 'Don't say someone else has gone missing.'

'Yes,' she said. 'I wonder if you've seen this girl?'

She showed them a photo of a pretty girl in a dancing
pose.

'That looks like a stage photo,' Lyn said. 'Yes, it's got the
name of the studio on the back. I went there for my stage
photos.'

Jed looked at the picture. For a split second, he paused.
'Never seen her. I wouldn't forget a nice girl like that.
What's her name?'

'Amy Peters. No one has seen her since Tuesday. Not
since she got off the bus just here. She came to dance in
the Seaside Show that starts next week.'

Lyn's blood ran cold. 'Just like me,' she said.

5

Jed walked with Lyn along the sea front to a large white guest house.

'Here it is,' he said, as he pointed to its lit-up name board.

'Is that really what it's called? Sweet Dreams Guest House!' Lyn giggled. 'I suppose it makes a change from Sea View!'

Steps led up to a large red door. Jed ran up. 'Come up here out of the rain.'

They both stood in the porch. Jed pressed the doorbell. It rang the tune of a lullaby. 'Sweet dreams indeed,' he said. 'Don't be put off by Mrs Burke. She's all right really. Her eggs and bacon are magic.'

The door opened and there stood a little old lady. She wore a smart blue suit. Her white hair was permed, with a hint of blue in it. She wore a string of pearls and looked very serious. 'Hi, Mrs Burke,' Jed said. 'I've got a nice young lady here. She's looking for a roof over her head.'

Mrs Burke leaned forward and looked Lyn up and down. 'Nice to meet you, dear. I've got a single room just right for you. It's no smoking and you have to be out by ten o'clock each morning. Come in.'

'Thanks,' said Lyn. Jed carried one of her bags into the long hallway. It was dark inside, with a faint smell of kippers. The slow tick-tock of a grandfather clock filled the hall.

Mrs Burke continued. 'No hot water after midnight. No guests in bedrooms. Nice face.'

'Sorry?' Lyn looked puzzled.

'You've got a very pretty face, my dear. And so slim. Just right, eh Jed? Now, I'll just make us all a nice cup of tea while you show Amy to her room.'

'Lyn. My name's Lyn.' There was an awkward silence.

'Lyn's in the show. She's a singer and dancer,' Jed said.

'That's nice, dear. Come down for tea in five minutes.'

Jed led the way up two flights of stairs. He took Lyn across a landing and down a dark hallway.

'Here you are. Room 14. Make yourself at home. Nice view over the sea. Sweet dreams! I'll come back for you in five minutes.' Jed left her at the door.

Lyn went into the small musty room. Dark red curtains hung at a small window. The view from it was grey sea and sky. She sat on the high old-fashioned bed. There was dark blue wallpaper on three walls. A picture on the fourth wall was a sea scene. It was grey. A large old wardrobe loomed at the foot of the bed.

Lyn gave a sigh. She didn't like this room. It had a strange feeling. But that wasn't all. There were two questions she had to answer. The first was simple. Why had Mrs Burke just called her Amy?

6

Lyn washed her face at the small sink in the corner of the room. There was a knock on the door. 'Hi, Lyn. It's Jed. Ready?'

Lyn opened the door. 'Why did she call me Amy? That's the name of the missing girl. The one in the photo the policewoman showed us.'

Jed didn't seem to make a lot of it. 'Well, you do look a bit alike.'

'But how did Mrs Burke know that? She didn't see the photo.'

'Local TV. Amy's face is all over the place. Easy mistake.'

Lyn wasn't so sure. She felt there was something strange about this house. It would be far from sweet dreams for her.

'And another question,' she began as they stood at the top of the stairs. 'How did you know which room to bring me to? I mean, there are lots of rooms in this house. You didn't have to ask her where to bring me. You knew the way like the back of your hand. How come?'

Jed didn't have time to answer. Lyn's foot slipped off the top stair. She fell with a scream and crashed to the bottom stair. She lay in a twisted heap and groaned.

Mrs Burke appeared as if from nowhere. 'My dear, you must be more careful. Let us help you up. Come and sit down in this room. Can you get up?'

Lyn was in a daze. She had banged her head badly. Her ankle was twisted. Jed helped her up and led her into an empty bedroom. Mrs Burke stood at the door. 'Just sit on the bed, my dear. Sip this tea and let me look at that ankle. Jed, I think you should call the doctor. Lyn must get that ankle seen to. You can't dance on that, can you my dear?'

Lyn was still in shock. She needed to rest. She needed to think. She just wanted to get away from this house.

'Now just lie down, dear. Try to rest. Sweet dreams, eh? Doctor Knox will soon be here. We'll look after you. Oh yes, we'll look after you all right . . .'

7

Lyn slept. Her mind spun in a deep dream. She could hear voices. She tried to wake up but a wave of sleep washed over her. Her dreams were far from sweet.

'She'll sleep for a while,' Dr Knox said. 'She's just like the last one. Just right. I'll get a DNA test on this blood sample and we'll find a match. Are you sure no one saw you bring her here?'

'You know me by now,' Jed said. 'Have I ever let you down? Not a soul saw us. And my little trick with the stair carpet never fails. It works every time. She fell from top to bottom. Magic. So how much will you pay us for this one?'

'That depends,' Dr Knox said. 'If we can use all her organs, you'll get a good price. Maybe twenty thousand. She's fit and young. You've done well. The last one was good, too.'

'Amy took a long time to kill,' Mrs Burke spoke. 'She put up quite a fight. Jed had to hold the pillow on her face for a good five minutes. You didn't drug her enough.'

'It's risky. I have to be careful,' the doctor said. 'I can't use much or it will affect her organs. We want them in perfect shape. At the moment we've got an important MP and a judge both waiting for a new liver. And a big pop star. We need some new parts fast. I hope Lyn's will be a good match. There could be big money in it for all of us.'

'That's good,' Mrs Burke said as she poured a cup of tea. 'I'd like to paint this room. It could do with a new colour. It costs such a lot these days. It's not easy running a guest house like this, you know.'

8

Lyn woke in a daze. Her head was in a swirl. Her heart thumped. Her ankle throbbed. She wasn't sure why, but she knew she was in great danger. She just had to get out of this room. Where was she?

The room was dark. The house was still. She had to pull herself from sleep. But she longed to lie back again and drift away. No, she had to fight it. She had to get out of this house.

She was aware of a smell. It was musty. Smoky, like kippers.

The smell began to bring it all back to her. It started her thinking. Could she remember? Voices. She had heard voices. Somewhere in the back of her mind . . . there were voices. She'd heard a doctor. She'd heard Jed. Jed – someone she'd trusted. Someone she'd thought was a friend. She'd heard that creepy old woman, who spoke about killing someone.

Lyn dragged herself out of bed. She crawled towards the misty red light at the window. With all her strength, she pulled back the curtains. Air. She had to get some air. She fumbled with the window catch. At last it opened and a salty breeze blew in.

She sucked cool air into her lungs. Cold, sweet air. All she could see out there in the murky light of morning was a milky fog hanging over the same grey sea.

A gull screamed somewhere in the mist. Lyn looked at her watch. It was ten past seven. The street below was quiet. Nothing moved on the beach.

Slowly her memory came back to her. The bus. The café. Jed Hare. Amy. Strange questions. Sweet Dreams Guest House. Mrs Burke. Falling. Voices in the night. Dr Knox. Her eyes stared round the gloomy room. She was back in Room 14. Her bags had gone. There was no sign of her mobile phone.

Lyn looked in the wardrobe. Its door swung open with a creak. There was a stale smell of mothballs. She pulled open a small drawer. There was a book hidden inside. Lyn took it out and a photo fell from it. She picked it up and stared at it for almost a full minute. She had seen that face before. Where? She was tired and her mind was numb.

It was just like the photo the policewoman showed her of Amy Peters. There was writing on the back. Lyn could just make out the words: 'Help. I think they're going to kill me. Amy.'

Lyn felt faint . . . and sick. She opened her bedroom door and looked outside. The house was still. She heard the grandfather clock chime down in the hall. She had to get down to it and find the front door.

Bacon was cooking in the kitchen. The smell made her think of home. It used to be a comforting smell. Not now. Lyn thought of Mrs Burke frying liver and bacon. Or kidneys. The thought made her feel sick. This was the house of the body snatchers.

Lyn's legs gave way as she got to the front door. She was sure she'd been drugged. Her mind was in a thick fog. But it was clear enough to remember a film she'd seen once. A film about a pair of body snatchers in the nineteenth century. They were an evil pair who sold bodies to a doctor. And now Lyn thought of their names. Burke and Hare.

It seemed they had returned . . .

9

The heavy mist rolled in from the sea. It wrapped the coast road in a thick blanket of fog. Lyn fell out of the front door of Sweet Dreams Guest House. She clung to the rails down the steps and sank to her knees in the street. Deathly silence. The mist closed around her.

Lyn knew she had to get away fast. She had to put that place behind her. She'd get help as soon as she was safe. She'd tell them about the evil things inside Sweet Dreams Guest House.

She could hardly walk. Step by step she limped along the foggy street. She'd try to find the pier again. She'd try to find a phone. She just had to tell someone . . . quickly.

Lyn could hear waves lapping over the shingle. She could hear gulls calling above the sea. But her mind was in a spin. How she wanted to sleep! To close her eyes and escape. She made herself keep walking. Step after step. But where was she? She had no idea. Her head was in a fog. Her eyes were in a fog. Her world was in a fog. She had no energy left. Every step drained her. But still she put one foot in front of the other.

At last, Lyn saw a faint light in the mist. It was still early but someone might be there. She struggled on. Yes, it was the café by the pier.

She had no energy left. Time and again she fell off the kerb. It felt like she had heavy flu. 'It must be the drugs,' she thought. 'I've got to get medical help.' Once more she fell in the road.

A woman in curlers poked her head out of an upstairs window. 'It looks like you've had a great all-night party, love. How much booze have you had?' Her cackles filled the street.

Lyn looked up and called feebly. 'Can you call me an ambulance?'

'That's not all I'll call you, dear! I'll call you a dirty stop-out who can't take her drink. Get back to bed, love. Sleep it off.'

'Please!' Lyn begged. 'I need help. Get me an ambulance.'

The woman pulled her dressing gown round her shoulders. She said something that Lyn couldn't hear and shut the window. Lyn could only stagger on to the pier café.

The lights were on. Help wasn't far away. She just had to get to that light. Lyn forced herself to keep going. She crossed the street and fell over the kerb. She crawled up to the door.

Inside, a girl was mopping the floor. Lyn pushed the door open and fell inside. The girl looked up in surprise.

'Sorry, we're not open yet.' Lyn got to her feet and held on to one of the tables.

'Please. You've got to help me!' She fell on to a chair and sobbed.

10

'You'd better sit down,' the girl said. 'Are you all right?'

Lyn tried to calm down. But the relief was too much. 'Please,' she sobbed, 'can you make a phone call for me?'

'Sure. No problem. Listen, let me get you a cup of something.'

'Not yet. First you must call the police. Just tell them to get here as fast as they can. I've got to tell them . . .'

The girl stared at Lyn for a few seconds.

'All right, love. Don't worry. I've got a phone in the office. I won't be long. Just sit down and relax.' She left her mop and went into a room at the back.

Lyn sighed. The relief. It seemed as if a huge weight was being lifted from her shoulders. She sat with her head in her hands, trying to make sense of the last few hours. She heard the girl's voice on the phone. It wouldn't be long now. Her mind began to sink into sleep.

Doubts filled her head. Had she made it all up? Was she just being stupid? Could she prove anything? Questions crashed round her mind. Maybe it was all a bad dream.

Maybe those sweet dreams had just gone sour. Maybe she just had a nasty dose of flu and wasn't thinking straight.

The girl's voice brought Lyn back to her senses.

'Don't worry,' she said. 'I've made the call. Drink this and relax.'

A mug of hot coffee steamed in front of her. 'They won't be long now,' the girl smiled.

Lyn drank in big gulps. She hadn't eaten for ages. She needed something to wake her up. The room was a blur.

A few cars moved slowly past the window. A postman rode his bike down the street and vanished into the fog. A van brought a bundle of newspapers. The world carried on just the same. No one knew a thing.

Suddenly Lyn saw a dark shape coming through the mist. It was the shape of a person. At last. Would this be the policewoman she'd seen the day before? The door opened and the dark figure stood in the doorway. It looked straight at Lyn. Her heart missed a beat. It was Jed.

'Hi, Lyn. I've come to take you back. You left your bags. You can't run off like that. Not without paying. Come on. You look so sleepy. You need to come back with me – right now.'

The girl with the mop smiled and kissed Jed on the lips. 'It's funny how a few sleeping pills in a coffee can work so quick,' she said. 'I popped in some extra strong ones, Jed.'

He smiled and stroked her cheek. Lyn sighed. The room was spinning. She felt sick inside. The girl spoke again.

'Jed, the next bus comes in at midday. I'll call you when another little stranger turns up all alone, eh?'

Jed smiled. 'Sure. Magic.'

Lyn felt a knot tighten in the pit of her stomach. Was this still part of her nightmare? She looked into Jed's eyes. They didn't sparkle now. His eyes were hard and cold.

'And don't forget the mobile-jammer,' he told the girl. 'Switch it on as soon as the bus comes in. It worked a treat with Lyn's mobile. It knocked out the signal just right. She was putty in our hands, weren't you, Lyn?'

Lyn tried to scream. No sound came out. Her eyes closed. Her tears fell to the floor. She laid her head on the table with a groan.

The girl kissed Jed again. 'Are you pleased with me, Jed?'

'Yeah, magic!' Jed laughed. 'That's what I call real magic.'

He whispered in Lyn's ear. 'Sweet dreams, my dear. Sweet dreams . . .'

Her dreams weren't at all sweet. They were full of voices. Noises. Sirens. She tried to fight. She had to wake up. Yes, it was a siren. She opened her eyes. A blue light flashed out in the street. It was an ambulance. The woman at the window must have phoned for an ambulance after all!

Jed and the girl were in the office. This was Lyn's chance. She pulled herself to her feet. Her head was swimming but she had to get out. She threw herself at the door and pulled it open. The cool damp air gave her new strength. She ran as if she was drunk, towards the ambulance. She waved her arms. 'Help me! Please take me away.'

Two men stood with a stretcher behind the ambulance.

'Are you all right, miss?' one called to her.

She fell at his feet. 'Please help. I'm in danger. They've drugged me.'

'It's all right, love. Tell us all about it. Just lie down on the stretcher and we'll take you away and sort you out.'

She looked behind her and saw Jed walking towards them.

'Quick. You've got to get me away from him.'

'Don't worry, love. Just relax,' one of the men said as they picked her up on the stretcher. As they slid her inside the ambulance she felt safe at last. 'We'll look after you. Don't worry.'

She closed her eyes and gave a sigh. She felt a cold hand on her brow. 'Just get some rest, my dear. Try to sleep.'

It was a voice she knew. The voice in her nightmare. The voice of Dr Knox.

Lyn opened her eyes. The doctor was looking down at her and smiling. Jed was now standing beside him. 'Nice to see you, Dr Knox. She ran straight into your arms, I see.'

'Indeed,' the doctor said. 'And I will need to inject her one last time . . .'

Jed smiled. 'Still warm . . . and fresh. Dead fresh! Magic.'

The ambulance doors slammed shut. Lyn heard no more as its engine rumbled to life. Her world was dark and silent once more.

Outside the mist crept slowly round the beach huts. It drifted like heavy smoke over a pile of damp deckchairs. Grey rain blew in once more from a grey and silent sea . . .

31